GOSCINNY AND UDERZO
PRESENT
AN ASTERIX ADVENTURE

ASTERIX AND SON

WRITTEN AND ILLUSTRATED BY UDERZO
TRANSLATED BY ANTHEA BELL AND DEREK HOCKRIDGE

HODDER AND STOUGHTON

LONDON   SYDNEY   AUCKLAND   TORONTO

British Library Cataloguing in Publication Data

Goscinny, René
  Asterix and Son
  I. Title   II. Uderzo, Albert
  741.5'944   PN6747

  ISBN 0-340-33008-2 (cased)
  ISBN 0-340-35331-7 (paperbound)

**Original edition: © Editions Albert René,
Goscinny-Uderzo, 1983**
English translation: © Editions Albert René,
Goscinny-Uderzo, 1983
Exclusive licensee: Hodder and Stoughton Ltd
Translators: Anthea Bell and Derek Hockridge

First published in Great Britain 1983 (cased)
Third impression 1984

First published in Great Britain 1985 (paperbound)

Printed in Belgium for Hodder and Stoughton Children's Books,
a division of Hodder and Stoughton Ltd,
Mill Road, Dunton Green, Sevenoaks, Kent TN13 2YJ
by Henri Proost & Cie, Turnhout

GAULISH VILLAGE

COMPENDIUM

LAUDANUM

AQUARIUM

TOTORUM

ARMORICA

BELGICA

LUTETIA

GAUL
(ROMAN CONQUEST)
50 B.C.

CELTICA

PROVINCIA

AQUITANIA

SPQR

The year is 50 BC. Gaul is entirely occupied by the Romans. Well, not entirely... One small village of indomitable Gauls still holds out against the invaders. And life is not easy for the Roman legionaries who garrison the fortified camps of Totorum, Aquarium, Laudanum and Compendium...

a few of the Gauls

Asterix, the hero of these adventures. A shrewd, cunning little warrior; all perilous missions are immediately entrusted to him. Asterix gets his superhuman strength from the magic potion brewed by the druid Getafix...

Obelix, Asterix's inseparable friend. A menhir delivery-man by trade, addicted to wild boar. Obelix is always ready to drop everything and go off on a new adventure with Asterix – so long as there's wild boar to eat, and plenty of fighting. His constant companion is Dogmatix, the only known canine ecologist, who howls with despair when a tree is cut down.

Getafix, the venerable village druid. Gathers mistletoe and brews magic potions. His speciality is the potion which gives the drinker superhuman strength. But Getafix also has other recipes up his sleeve...

Cacofonix, the bard. Opinion is divided as to his musical gifts. Cacofonix thinks he's a genius. Everyone else thinks he's unspeakable. But so long as he doesn't speak, let alone sing, everybody likes him...

Finally, Vitalstatistix, the chief of the tribe. Majestic, brave and hot-tempered, the old warrior is respected by his men and feared by his enemies. Vitalstatistix himself has only one fear, he is afraid the sky may fall on his head tomorrow. But as he always says, 'Tomorrow never comes.'

THE SUN IS RISING OVER ASTERIX'S VILLAGE, AS USUAL. THE SCENE IS ONE OF PEACE AND SERENITY...

...DISTURBED, DESPITE THE FACT THAT DAY IS DAWNING, BY THE SNORES OF THE ONLY GAULISH ROOSTER WHO HAS ADENOIDS.

SNORT! ZZZ!

IT'S COCKCROW, YOU GOOSE! TIME TO TALK TURKEY.

YOU'RE IN A FOWL MOOD THIS MORNING!

TAP! TAP! TAP!

COCK-A-DOODLE-DOO

YAWN!

COME ON, GET UP! IT'S GOING TO BE A LOVELY DAY!

I HAD SUCH A FUNNY DREAM LAST NIGHT, ASTERIX!

SCRATCH! SCRATCH!

I DREAMED THE STORKS VISITED OUR VILLAGE, BRINGING THE BABIES PEOPLE HAD ORDERED, AND ONE OF THEM LEFT A BABY HERE BY MISTAKE!

SCRATCH SCRATCH!

DON'T SAY YOU STILL BELIEVE STORKS DELIVER BABIES!

WHY NOT? I DELIVER MENHIRS, DON'T I?

ONE OF THESE DAYS YOU AND I MUST HAVE A LITTLE TALK, OBELIX!

CREEEAK

GA! GA!

?

GOO! GOO!

GURGLE!

5

8

CHIEF VITALSTATISTIX, WHAT AM I GOING TO DO ABOUT THIS BABY?

CLUCK!

DON'T YOU THINK YOU'VE DONE ENOUGH ALREADY?

AND DON'T TOUCH THAT CHILD WITH YOUR CLUMSY GREAT HANDS! WHAT HE NEEDS IS A MOTHER'S TENDER CARE!

DON'T YOU, MY LITTLE SWEETIE-PIE?

GA?

POC!

?

YOU COME HOME WITH ME! AND IN FUTURE, I DON'T WANT YOU MIXING WITH PEOPLE WHOSE EFFECT ON ALL AROUND THEM IS SO DEVASTATING!

BUT IMPEDIMENTA, DEAR...

?

CLUCK!

I THINK THIS BABY HAS HIS HEAD SCREWED ON THE RIGHT WAY!

GA!

WELL, THAT SETTLES IT, ASTERIX!

HE'S DEFINITELY PICKED YOU TWO FOR HIS ADOPTIVE FATHERS!

ASTERIX AND OBELIX, THE GUARDIANSHIP OF THIS CHILD, WITH ALL ITS WEIGHTY RESPONSIBILITIES, IS NOW YOURS. TAKE GOOD CARE OF HIM!

I WILL NOW GIVE YOU AN ODE ON THE JOYS OF FAMILY LIFE!

YOU TRY IT!

HE'S GONE TO SLEEP! NO BIGGER THAN A WILD BOAR PIGLET, AND HE'S AS MUCH TROUBLE AS MAKING FIFTY MENHIRS!

WHO ON EARTH CAN HAVE BEEN BOLD ENOUGH TO ABANDON THIS BABY?

I TOLD YOU. IT MUST HAVE BEEN A STORK WHO...

SHUT UP ABOUT STORKS, OR I SHALL DO YOU AN INJURY!

SSSSH! YOU'LL WAKE HIM UP, AND THEN HE'LL WANT A COW TO RATTLE!

THAT'S WHAT COMES OF BEING FOOL ENOUGH TO GIVE HIM A BOTTLE OF MILK WITH MAGIC POTION IN IT!

HARK AT MISTER ASTERIX! FULL OF THE MILK OF HUMAN KINDNESS, AREN'T YOU? WHO'S A MILKSOP, THEN?

MILKSOP YOURSELF! IT'S YOUR SOPPY FAULT!

OH, REALLY? YOU DON'T BELIEVE IN BOTTLING UP A GRIEVANCE DO YOU?

YOU'RE ENOUGH TO MAKE ME TAKE TO THE BOTTLE MYSELF!

WAAAAA!

!

WAAAH!

THERE! WHAT DID I TELL YOU?

I THINK IT'S HIGH TIME WE WENT IN SEARCH OF THAT BABY'S PARENTS!

SO A LITTLE LATER...

ASTERIX, HOW ARE WE GOING TO RECOGNIZE PARENTS WHO WON'T EVEN RECOGNIZE THEIR OWN CHILD?

WE DO HAVE ONE CLUE: THE BABY'S CLOTHES AND WRAPPINGS ARE MADE OF EMBROIDERED LINEN, THE SORT OF THING YOU'D EXPECT TO FIND IN A RICH ROMAN FAMILY...

SO WE'LL START BY INVESTIGATING THE FORTIFIED ROMAN CAMPS THAT SURROUND THE VILLAGE!

OH, GOODY! I LOVE INVESTIGATING ROMAN CAMPS!

DOGMATIX, YOU GUARD THAT BABY WHILE WE'RE OUT! IF ANYONE COMES NEAR HIM, EAT THEM. UNDERSTAND?

DO YOU REALLY THINK DOGMATIX IS UP TO IT?

WOOF!

OF COURSE! HE'S HAD LOTS OF EXPERIENCE. I'VE TAUGHT HIM TO GUARD MENHIRS!

MEANWHILE, AT CONDATUM, IN THE RESIDENCE OF THE PREFECT OF ARMORICA...

QUICK! SEND A MESSENGER OFF TO ROME!

DON'T BOTHER, CACTUS!

BRUTUS!?

THAT'S RIGHT! I'VE COME FROM ROME SPECIALLY TO HEAR THE LATEST ABOUT OUR LITTLE AFFAIR!

JUDGING BY YOUR SLOVENLY APPEARANCE, CONTACT WITH THE LOCAL BARBARIANS IS BAD FOR YOU!

CONTACT WITH THEIR FISTS IS! THIS INVESTIGATION YOU WANTED MADE IS A RISKY BUSINESS!

HAVE YOU FOUND THE BABY?

YES, I HAVE. HE'S IN A LITTLE VILLAGE ON THE NORTH COAST... BUT GUARDED BY TWO FIERCE GAULS WHO FLATTENED AN ENTIRE INFANTRY SECTION!

HMM... CAESAR'S OFTEN TOLD ME ABOUT THAT VILLAGE OF CRAZY BUT INDOMITABLE GAULS WHO GET THEIR STRENGTH FROM DRINKING MAGIC POTION!

13A

BUT I'LL HAVE THAT BABY EVEN IF I HAVE TO PUT ALL GAUL TO FIRE AND THE SWORD!!!

LUCKILY, SOME WAY OFF...

COME ON, SON, TRY YOUR LEGS OUT!

GA!

LOOK, ASTERIX! HE KNOWS HIS HOME ALREADY!

BANG!

?!

JUST LIKE ME AT HIS AGE!

I WONDER IF WE'RE SETTING THAT CHILD A GOOD EXAMPLE?

AGA!

13B

LATER... WELL, THE DOOR'S REPAIRED, THE BABY'S ASLEEP, AND DOGMATIX IS ON GUARD. SO LET'S GO AND DISCUSS THE SITUATION WITH CHIEF VITALSTATISTIX!

I'VE GOT TO DELIVER A MENHIR TO BUCOLIX FIRST!

MENHIRS HAVE A LONG SHELF LIFE... CAN'T IT WAIT?

NO, IT CAN'T. I ALWAYS MAKE SURE MY MENHIRS ARE SHIFTED BEFORE THE "SELL BY" DATE!

SO THE ROMANS KNOW THE BABY IS HERE, AND THIS FAKE CENSUS OF THEIRS SUGGESTS THAT THEIR INTENTIONS AREN'T ENTIRELY HONOURABLE!

BUT WE STILL DON'T KNOW WHY SOMEONE CHOSE OUR VILLAGE AS THE PLACE TO LEAVE THE BABY.

I THINK I KNOW WHY!

THE BABY MUST NEED PROTECTION FROM THE ROMANS... AND OUR VILLAGE IS THE ONE SAFE PLACE WHERE ROMANS WOULD NEVER DARE TO COME!

CRAAASH! ? ?

ASTERIX, SINCE I'M GOING TO SEE BUCOLIX ANYWAY, WOULD YOU LIKE ME TO PICK UP ANOTHER COW FOR THE LITTLE LAD?

OBELIX, MY BOY, I WISH TO GOODNESS YOU'D TAKE YOUR MENHIR OFF WHEN YOU COME INDOORS!

BUT, CHIEF, MENHIRS ARE HIGH FASHION INDOORS AS WELL AS OUT!

TOO HIGH FOR *MY DOOR* BY HALF, YOU *IDIOT!*

BUT IN CONDATUM...

SO NOW YOU KNOW THE DREADFUL SECRET OF THAT CHILD'S BIRTH, CACTUS!

AND YOU ALSO KNOW THE EQUALLY DREADFUL SECRET OF MY PLAN! IF YOU BETRAY ME, IT WILL BE THE WORSE FOR YOU!

WHAT, ME, BETRAY YOU? DO I LOOK LIKE A TRAITOR?

YES! BUT I HAVE NO CHOICE. SO IF YOU SERVE ME WELL, YOU'LL GET THAT SEAT IN THE ROMAN SENATE YOU'VE BEEN WANTING SO LONG!

I'D SELL MY MOTHER AND FATHER TO SERVE YOU IF I HAVEN'T DONE THAT ALREADY, O BRUTUS, SON OF CAESAR!

ONLY ADOPTED SON OF CAESAR, AND ALL I'M ASKING YOU TO DO IS BRING ME THAT BABY!

I HAVE AN IDEA!

FLOP!

WAAAH!

ASTERIX, SUPPOSE I GAVE HIM JUST ONE TINY DROP OF MAGIC POTION, MAYBE HE'D...

YOU'LL DO NO SUCH THING! YOU TWO HAVE CREATED ENOUGH HAVOC ALREADY!!!

ALL RIGHT, ALL RIGHT, I GET THE IDEA! MUSTN'T TREAT THIS PLACE LIKE HOME, MUST WE, DOGMATIX?

WAAAAH!

HEY... HE'S LEFT ME HOLDING THE BABY! OH, VERY CLEVER, MISTER OBELIX!

WAAAH!

MEANWHILE, NOT FAR FROM THE VILLAGE...

O MARCUS JUNIUS BRUTUS, SINCE WE WANT OUR HQ NEAR THE INDOMITABLE GAULS, WHY DON'T WE USE ONE OF THE FORTIFIED CAMPS SURROUNDING THEIR VILLAGE?

BECAUSE CAESAR MIGHT GET TO HEAR OF IT, AND I'M NONE TO KEEN TO HAVE HIM ASKING ME WHAT I'M DOING HERE IN ARMORICA!

HALT! WE WILL PITCH CAMP HERE!

AND ONCE AGAIN WE ARE PRIVILEGED TO WATCH THE MANOEUVRES OF THE ROMAN ARMY. WHILE THE SAPPERS DIG A FOSSA (DITCH) AND RAISE AN AGGER (RAMPART)...

...THE WOODCUTTERS GO TO CHOP DOWN TREES...

...FOR THE CARPENTERS TO BUILD THE VALLUM (FENCE).

AT LAST THE CAMP IS READY. THE GENERAL AND HIS MEN ARE ABOUT TO ENTER IN REVIEW ORDER, THUS SYMBOLIZING THE MIGHT OF THE ROMAN ARMY, THE BEST-DISCIPLINED FIGHTING FORCE IN THE WORLD...

?

...ALTHOUGH SOMETIMES...

WHAT'S THAT?

MY TENT! I CAN'T STAND THE WAY THE OTHERS SNORE IN BED!

* ROMAN HEAD.

21 A

21 B

26

PAF!

YOU KNOW, RATTLING PEDLARS ISN'T VERY NICE!

GA!

I'M TERRIBLY SORRY!

THAT'S OKAY! I SORT OF LOVE KIDDIES, Y'KNOW!

WE STILL HAVE TO SOLVE THE PROBLEM. IF ONLY WE COULD TAKE HIM OUT HUNTING BOARS WITH US... BUT HE MIGHT COME HOME AND THUMP ALL THE VILLAGE ANIMALS!

YOU MUST GET AROUND THE COUNTRY-SIDE A LOT, AROMATIX. MAYBE YOU KNOW A NURSEMAID WHO'D BE BRAVE AND STRONG ENOUGH TO COME AND LOOK AFTER THIS BABY?

SURE! BUT IF, LIKE, YOU'RE SORT OF BUSY, WHY DON'T I LOOK AFTER HIM MYSELF FOR A WHILE, JUST TO HELP OUT, Y'KNOW?

YOU THINK WE OUGHT TO TAKE THE RISK, OBELIX?

IT'S THE PEDLAR WHO'D BE TAKING A RISK!

234

WELL, FINE, BUT MIND HE DOESN'T GET OUT OF THE HUT! WE'LL BE BACK QUITE SOON!

WE'RE ONLY GOING TO PICK OFF TWO OR THREE BOARS IN THE FOREST FOR SUPPER THIS EVENING!

I THINK THAT PEDLAR'S A RATTLING GOOD SORT TO AMUSE THE BABY, DON'T YOU, ASTERIX?

BANG! OUCH! PAF! OW!

GA?

I WONDER IF, LIKE, THE LIONS IN THE CIRCUS MIGHT HAVE, SORT OF, BEEN A BETTER BET!

LATER...

HE'S ASLEEP AT LAST! NOW TO GET HIM OUT OF THE CAMP BEFORE HE WAKES UP!

235

28

NOW, DRINK THIS PICK-ME-UP AND TELL US WHAT HAPPENED, ODORIFERUS!

I, LIKE, SORT OF WON THE GAULS' CONFIDENCE, Y'KNOW, AND THEY GAVE ME THE BABY TO LOOK AFTER...

I WAS GOING TO CARRY HIM OFF WHILE THEY WERE OUT, BUT THAT LITTLE MONSTER HAS, LIKE SUPERHUMAN STRENGTH, Y'KNOW, AND WHENEVER HE SEES ME HE SORT OF GOES INTO THE SAME ROUTINE, HE TAKES ME FOR A RATTLE AND...

HERE WE GO AGAIN!

EVEN THE GAULISH VILLAGERS ARE HAVING TROUBLE WITH HIM. ASTERIX HIMSELF ASKED IF I KNEW A NURSEMAID BRAVE AND STRONG ENOUGH TO LOOK AFTER HIM!

DID HE REALLY?

I THINK I'VE, LIKE, EARNED PROMOTION TO OPTIO!

YOU? YOU'VE FAILED IN YOUR MISSION. THINK YOURSELF LUCKY NOT TO BE SERVED UP TO THE LIONS IN THE CIRCUS MAXIMUS!

I DIDN'T, LIKE, KNOW THESE PARTS BEFORE, BUT I WON'T BE SORT OF FORGETTING THE DISCOVERY OF ARMORICA IN A HURRY!

WHAT HE SAID ABOUT THE NURSEMAID GAVE ME AN IDEA! WHY DON'T WE SEND ONE TO THE VILLAGE?

PAF!

BECAUSE WE HAVEN'T GOT ANY NURSEMAIDS IN THE ARMY, THAT'S WHY!

26

YES, WE HAVE... YOU!

WHAT DO YOU MEAN, ME?

THINK, CACTUS! THAT LUNATIC OF YOURS WAS WELL AND TRULY PUT THROUGH IT BY THE GAULS. WE MUST REMAIN THE ONLY ONES IN THE SECRET. AND IF YOU REALLY WANT THAT SEAT IN THE SENATE...

WELL, PROMISE ME NO ONE WILL GET TO KNOW, ANYWAY!

LATER...

AVE, GORGEOUS! LIKE A BIT OF SLAP AND TICKLE?

SLAP!

BY ZHUPITER! THAT'SH GOING A BIT TOO FAR!

IT WORKS! EVEN THE SENTRY WAS TAKEN IN!

26

(FALSETTO) MY NAME IS ASPIDISTRA, AND I HEARD YOU WERE LOOKING FOR A NURSE. I'M A VERY EXPERIENCED NURSEMAID!

?!

BUT YOU'RE NOT ONE OF OUR VILLAGERS ... HOW DID YOU KNOW I WAS LOOKING FOR A NURSE?

(FALSETTO) OH, THESE THINGS GET AROUND THE LEGION ... I MEAN THE REGION! SPECIALLY WHEN IT'S SOMETHING TO DO WITH THE BOLD AND FAMOUS WARRIOR ASTERIX!

!?

HOW ABOUT ME? DO THEY KNOW ABOUT *ME* IN THE REGION?

?

(FALSETTO) CAN I REALLY BE SPEAKING TO OBELIX, THE HANDSOME AND SEDUCTIVE MENHIR DELIVERY MAN?

HOWEVER DID YOU GUESS?

AND DID YOU ALSO HEAR THAT THE CHILD IN QUESTION IS ... ER ... RATHER A HANDFUL?

(FALSETTO) I'VE THUMPED ... THAT'S TO SAY, I'VE BROUGHT UP WORSE HANDFULS, I'M SURE!

284

WE CAN ALWAYS TRY. GO ON, THEN, BUT DON'T SAY I DIDN'T WARN YOU!

FUNNY ... I HAVE A FEELING I'VE SEEN HER FACE SOMEWHERE BEFORE!

MAYBE SHE'S NO MORE A NURSE THAN THAT MAN WAS A PEDLAR ... WHAT DO YOU THINK OF HER, OBELIX?

A WOMAN OF TASTE AND DISCERNMENT!

WOMAN OF TASTE OR NOT, WE'D BETTER WATCH OUT!

TCHAC!

I DID WARN YOU! HE'S IMPOSSIBLE!

OH, I'M NOT RATTLED! I GOT OFF TO A FLYING START!

285

UNDER THE LANTERNA, BY THE CASTRA*GATE... MY LILIUM OF THE LANTERNA LIGHT, MY OWN LILIUM MARLENA!

I DON'T THINK SHE'S MUCH BETTER THAN CACOFONIX!

BARBARIANS! YOU'RE ALL BARBARIANS!

LOOK, YOU CAN TELL THE BABY DOESN'T LIKE YOU MUCH!

A LITTLE LATER...

HE'S DROPPED OFF AGAIN! IT'S ALL RIGHT, YOU CAN LEAVE HIM TO ME NOW!

JUST ONE THING... HOW DO YOU COME TO KNOW THESE SOLDIERS' SONGS?

*LATIN: BARRACKS.

ER...A CHILDMINDER'S JOB DOESN'T PAY MUCH, SO I TOOK TO MINDING A ROMAN ARMY CANTEEN TOO. THERE ARE WAYS AND MEANS OF MOONLIGHTING, AND THAT'S MINE...

...AND THAT WAY I GOT TO BE A MINE OF INFORMATION ON THE ARMY!

OH, WON'T I JUST HAVE EARNED MY SEAT IN THE SENATE!

WAAAH!

WELL, YOU'RE NEEDED AS A CHILDMINDER NOW!

31 A

OH, OH, OH, IT'S A LOVELY BELLUM...

COME ON, OBELIX! LET'S FIND SOMEWHERE QUIETER!

OH, GOOD WORK, VITALSTATISTIX! MARVELLOUS, I CALL IT!

WHAT? WHAT HAVE I GONE AND DONE NOW?

YOU'RE CHIEF OF THIS VILLAGE... YOU LET A WOMAN FROM OUTSIDE COME AND LIVE UNDER A BACHELOR'S ROOF? OH, THAT'S GREAT!

BUT PEDIMENTA DEAR, SHE'S ONLY A NURSE FOR THE BABY!

EXACTLY! SUCH PROMISCUITY! SHOCKING!

I'M NOT ENJOYING THIS ADVENTURE VERY MUCH, OBELIX!

OH, IT'LL BE ALL RIGHT! IT'S SURE TO END WITH A BANQUET UNDER THE STARRY SKY, SAME AS USUAL!

31 B

NEXT MORNING...

OH, I **WILL** HAVE EARNED THAT SEAT IN THE SENATE, AND NO MISTAKE!

GLUG! GLUG! GLUG!

BUT FOR THE EFFECTS OF THAT WRETCHED POTION, I'D TUCK HIM UNDER MY ARM AND MAKE OFF WITH HIM NOW!

BURP!

PAT! PAT! PAT!

COME TO THINK OF IT, HOW DO I KNOW THE POTION'S STILL WORKING ON YOU, EH?

GA?

GA!

CLOCK!

33A

EVERYTHING OKAY?

SORT OF... ARE THE EFFECTS OF THAT MAGIC POTION GOING TO LAST MUCH LONGER?

THAT DEPENDS! JUDGING BY OBELIX, THEY COULD LAST FOR EVER!

AND SO, A LITTLE LATER...

WELL, I'M NOT GOING TO STICK AROUND IN THIS ROTTEN VILLAGE FOR EVER, WEARING THESE ROTTEN CLOTHES AND PLAYING THIS ROTTEN PART!

TOO BAD! I'LL RISK IT!

WHERE ARE YOU GOING, GORGEOUS?

ER...I'M GOING INTO THE FOREST TO PICK MUSHROOMS!

?

WAAAH!

33B

37

PACK UP YOUR TROUBLES IN YOUR OLD SARCINA* AND SMILE, SMILE, SMILE...♪

?!

SO NOW WE'RE OUT OF SIGHT OF THE VILLAGE...

*LATIN: KIT-BAG.

... I'LL MAKE STRAIGHT FOR THE CAMP!

WHERE ARE YOU GOING, OBELIX?

I'M DELIVERING A MENHIR TO BUCOLIX. THAT BABY HAS A GOOD APPETITE... HE'S COSTING US MANY A MENHIR!

I'LL COME WITH YOU!

I THOUGHT WE'D BE BETTER OFF WITH A NURSE. THEY USUALLY PROVIDE THE MILK, BUT THIS ONE DOESN'T SEEM TO.

34A

IF YOU'RE LOOKING FOR THE BABY AND HIS NURSE, THEY'VE GONE INTO THE FOREST TO PICK MUSHROOMS!

QUICK, OBELIX! I'VE GOT A NASTY FEELING...

KEEP MY MENHIR ON ICE, FOTOGENIX! WE SHAN'T BE VERY LONG!

OUF!

SNIFF! SNIFF!

PHEW! THAT'S A WEIGHT OFF MY MIND!

GA!

MY MIND?

THROWING YOUR WEIGHT AROUND, EH? WAIT TILL I CATCH YOU, YOU ☀%@º!※!

34B

HELP! HELP! SAVE ME!

YESH, BY ZHUPITER! COME TO MY...

...ARMS!

SPLATCH!

DON'T BE RIDICULOUS, CACTUS! I ORDER YOU TO COME DOWN!

PROMISE ME HE ISN'T IN THE CAMP!

TOO BAD! SO I WON'T GET TO BE SENATOR... BUT DON'T ANYONE EVER MENTION THAT MONSTER TO ME AGAIN!

NOW, NOW! WE'VE LOST A BATTLE, WE HAVEN'T LOST THE WAR!

I TOLD YOU I'D PUT ALL GAUL TO FIRE AND THE SWORD IF NECESSARY... *SO NOW LET'S LIGHT THE FIRE!!*

AND AT DUSK...

FANCY MAKING US HAUL THESE ROMAN RELICS UP, JUST TO SHOOT OFF A LOT OF FIERY ARROWS!

YES, IT'S A FLAMING NUISANCE!

ARE YOU REALLY GOING TO PUT ALL GAUL TO FIRE AND THE SWORD, BRUTUS?

WELL, THE VILLAGE OF THOSE INDOMITABLE GAULS WILL DO! I'M TOLD THE THATCH ON GAULISH HUTS BURNS FAST AND WELL.

THIS TIME THE ROMANS HAVE TURNED OUT MORE CUNNING AND PERSISTENT THAN USUAL!

SO WE MUST TAKE MORE CARE THAN USUAL!

AND GOSSIP LESS, TOO!

YOU *WOULD* KEEP A-HOLD OF NURSE AND YOU FOUND SOMETHING WORSE!

41

43

SO THEY ARE... AND AT DAWN...

COCK-A... COUGH-A... COUGH!

LOOK, ASTERIX! I'VE MET THE PEDLAR AGAIN!

AND I'VE MET THE NURSE!

IT'S A GOOD THING WE OUTNUMBER THEM, OR WE MIGHT HAVE BEEN MOVED!

PAF! PAF! PAF! PAF!

NOW, TELL ME WHAT REALLY BROUGHT YOU HERE, OR YOU'LL HAVE A FEW TROUBLES OF YOUR OWN TO PACK UP IN YOUR OLD SARCINA!

MERCY! I WAS ONLY OBEYING THE ORDERS OF CAESAR'S SON, BRUTUS!

AND WHERE IS BRUTUS?

ON THE BEACH! HE KNEW YOU'D SEND THE BABY TO SAFETY THERE!

QUICK, OBELIX! FOLLOW ME!

QUICK, DOGMATIX! FOLLOW US!

WOOF! WOOF!

WHERE'S THE BABY?

ASTERIX, I HAVE FAILED YOU! A ROMAN SNATCHED HIM AND TOOK HIM ON BOARD A PIRATE SHIP!

I CAN STILL SEE IT ON THE HORIZON!

DO YOU THINK YOU COULD SWIM OUT THAT FAR?

YOU REALLY DO ASK STUPID QUESTIONS SOMETIMES, ASTERIX!

SORRY. I WAS ONLY THINKING...

WELL, OF COURSE I CAN!

I DON'T KNOW WHAT I'D DO WITHOUT YOU, OBELIX!

ALL SORTS OF SILLY THINGS!

SPLOSH! SPLOSH! SPLOSH! SPL

CLEOPATRA!

?!

AMAZING! WHAT A SIGHT!

AND WHAT A NOSE!

MY SON? CAESARION? BUT I THOUGHT YOU WERE BOTH SAFE IN MY PALACE IN ROME!

DID YOU SAY SAFE?

AFTER YOU LEFT, THE VILLAINOUS BRUTUS MADE SEVERAL ATTEMPTS TO DO AWAY WITH CAESARION, HOPING TO BECOME SOLE HEIR TO YOUR PROPERTY AND YOUR FORTUNE!

SO I DECIDED TO SEND OUR SON AWAY TO THE ONE PLACE WHERE I COULD BE SURE HE WOULD BE SAFE: THE VILLAGE OF INDOMITABLE GAULS WHICH STILL HOLDS OUT AGAINST THE INVADERS!

ALL RIGHT, I KNOW!

ET TU, BRUTE?* YOU WILL LEAVE IMMEDIATELY FOR UPPER GERMANIA! IT HAS A NICE BRACING CLIMATE, AND THE BARBARIANS THERE WILL TEACH YOU MANNERS!

*YOU TOO, BRUTUS? CAESAR SOMETIMES REPEATED HIMSELF.

FORGIVE ME FOR TAKING ADVANTAGE OF YOU, ASTERIX!

OH, THAT'S ALL RIGHT! I'M HONOURED BY YOUR FAITH IN ME, QUEEN CLEOPATRA!

THE... THE BABY'S DISAPPEARED!

47

PRINTED IN BELGIUM BY
proost
INTERNATIONAL BOOK PRODUCTION